I0765555

HUGO THE PUPPY HERO

Elisabeth Davis

Copyright ©2023 Elisabeth Davis

All Rights Reserved

Dedication

To all of my family and especially Charlotte and Alicia and all their hopes and dreams.

Acknowledgements

Thanks to Harris, Oscar and Aiden for their support.

About The Author

Elisabeth Davis is a mum and granny who began writing stories at the age of 8 and achieved the Brownies writers badge. She has a lively and energetic dog named Hugo, who both frustrates and amuses her, but is beloved for his affectionate nature and inspiring qualities for writing. Elisabeth has spent many hours chasing after Hugo or smiling at his adventures, which have become a source of inspiration for her writing. Her latest story is the second in a series and is largely fictional, inspired by one of Hugo's real-life escapades..

In the space between being awake and sleeping is a special place where all the best stories are kept. This is a story about a puppy called Hugo.

Hugo is a happy, friendly dog, and everyone loves Hugo.

Hugo the puppy lived with Olivia and Oscar and Emma. At breakfast, Olivia was looking at her phone. 'Did you know dogs can smell things over 11 miles away? It says on my news feed.' They all looked at Hugo and chuckled as Hugo loved food and was always finding new things to sniff.

It was a lovely sunny day with blue skies, and Olivia was in the garden deadheading the dahlias and doing some weeding, and Emma was kicking the ball with Hugo, racing to catch it.

"Can Hugo come to the Park?" said Emma. Down the road was a big park, and Hugo loved to run and play and walk in the park.

"Not today. It's too hot for Hugo."

When Hugo heard the word 'Park' his tail swished back and forth and then stopped

PARK

Hugo loved going to the park. Could not somebody see that he was really, really bored and wanted to go on an adventure?

Dad and Emma walked down the road to the park, leaving Hugo behind. Olivia waved from the front garden and carried on weeding.

Hugo did help with the gardening. He dug some holes in the lawn and then dug out a plant and gave it a good shake. Then he pruned a stick from a tasty Weigelia shrub by chewing on it.

Hugo could smell the park and then saw the open gate and walked down the road to find Oscar and Emma in the park.

Olivia saw the end of his bushy tail as he walked through the front gate, that she had forgotten to shut, then he was off. "Stop Hugo" Olivia yelled, "come back." But it was too late. Hugo had been to the park many times and knew the way. Olivia was puffing behind.

Hugo walked quickly down the street, past the park cafe with the tables and chairs of pink and blue, past a family eating dripping ice cream, and right into the park.

Emma saw Hugo first as Hugo ran towards them. "Isn't that Hugo? What a surprise!" Hugo was delighted because he could NOW run around, and so he ran around the park several times, kicking a few footballs and smelling all the delicious smells in the park

Ice Cream
Park

Mr Jones looked like he was sunbathing. He lived next door and often called out "Hey Hugo," but today Hugo knew from his nose that Mr Jones wasn't well and he needed to help his friend. He grabbed his coat and tried to drag his friend onto the path where someone would find him, but this wouldn't work. He then let out a few growls and small urgent barks to try and get attention. And then barked very loudly.

Olivia and Oscar were still trying to catch Hugo, and with his barking, they could finally reach him. Then they saw Mr Jones lying on the floor looking very ill. When Olivia saw Mr Jones, she realised that he needed help very quickly as he had diabetes and had collapsed. She rang the emergency services and asked them to hurry.

woof
woof

The ambulance drove right into the park, and whilst the ambulance crew were helping Mr Jones, Oscar ex-plained that Hugo had found Mr Jones.

Olivia patted Hugo on the head and said, "You are a hero today. You have just saved Mr Jones with your clever nose. He was very ill, and you got there just in time." Olivia gave Hugo a great big hug and said, "Let's go home now and have dinner."

What a great day! Hugo was now having a great time as he ate his dinner and wagged his tail.

AMBULANCE

Then Mr Jones explained how Hugo the dog found him, the local papers wanted to print the story.

NEWS

The next day at Breakfast, a newspaper report was in Olivia's newsfeed on her mobile, which said,

"Hero dog saves Neighbour."

Olivia and Oscar and Emma were so proud of Hugo.

www.ingramcontent.com/pod-product-compliance
Lightning Source LLC
Chambersburg PA
CBHW080810020826
48982CB00018B/985

9 781916 798403